FRACTURED FAIRY TALES

SLEEPING BEAUTÉ

Graphic Planet

An Imprint of Magic Wagon
abdobooks.com

THIS BOOK IS DEDICATED TO THE WILDE FAMILY: BRANDON K., JESSICA, AEDAN, KAYLIE, WYATT AND AURORA!
LOVE IS LOVE. -AM

TO MY SON HEITOR, WHO LOVES WHAT I DO. AND TO MY WIFE JO, WHO WAS WITH ME UNTIL LATE AT NIGHT WHILE I ILLUSTRATED THIS BOOK. LOVE YOU GUYS. -LA

abdobooks.com

Published by Magic Wagon, a division of ABDO, PO Box 398166, Minneapolis, Minnesota 55439. Copyright © 2021 by Abdo Consulting Group, Inc. International copyrights reserved in all countries.
No part of this book may be reproduced in any form without written permission from the publisher. Graphic Planet™ is a trademark and logo of Magic Wagon.

Printed in the United States of America, North Mankato, Minnesota.
102020
012021

Written by Andy Mangels
Illustrated and Colored by Lelo Alves
Lettered by Kathryn S. Renta
Editorial supervision by David Campiti/MJ Macedo
Packaged by Glass House Graphics
Art Directed by Candice Keimig
Editorial Support by Bridget O'Brien

Library of Congress Control Number: 2020941555

Publisher's Cataloging-in-Publication Data

Names: Mangels, Andy, author. | Alves, Lelo, illustrator.
Title: Sleeping beauté / by Andy Mangels ; illustrated by Lelo Alves.
Description: Minneapolis, Minnesota : Magic Wagon, 2021. | Series: Fractured fairy tales
Summary: When Tay discovers that she's trapped in her favorite video game, she reaches out to help a troubled friend to figure out how to escape the virtual world.
Identifiers: ISBN 9781532139772 (lib. bdg.) | ISBN 9781098230050 (ebook) | ISBN 9781098230197 (Read-to-Me ebook)
Subjects: LCSH: Virtual reality--Juvenile fiction. | Video games and children--Juvenile fiction. | Friendship--Juvenile fiction. | Fairy tales--Juvenile fiction. | Escapes--Juvenile fiction. | Graphic novels—Juvenile fiction.
Classification: DDC 741.5--dc23

TABLE OF CONTENTS

I know the other kids think I'm fat, but I don't look forward to lunch for the food.

It's when I get to see my gamer friends IRL.

TAY, I HEAR YOU ZONKED OUT IN MATH CLASS?

YEP. FULL-ON DROOL AND EVERYTHING.

BUT I STILL GOT THE PROBLEM ON THE BOARD RIGHT!

NICE!

STEALTH SMART GIRL. YOU KNOW IT.

DID YOU GUYS SEE THE NEW AD FOR SKY EMPIRE AFTERSHOCK 4?

ONLY TWO MORE WEEKS UNTIL IT LAUNCHES!

Sky Empire Aftershock 4

DUH, HECTOR. LIKE, WHO DOESN'T KNOW WHEN --

HEY BEAUTY! WE NEED ANOTHER BIG GUY ON THE WRESTLING TEAM TO GO UP AGAINST THE BUCCANEERS NEXT MONTH.

YOU WANNA JOIN THE TEAM?

I DON'T THINK THE CYCLONES COULD HANDLE WHAT I GOT TO BRING, THAD.

I JUST BEAT A WEREWOLF THIS MORNING.

7

WEIRDO.

I ASSUME YOU MEAN A WEREWOLF IN CRAFTZONE ARENA, NOT LIKE WE'RE LIVING ABOVE A VORTEX OF DOOM OR SOMETHING?

DUH. THOUGH A VORTEX COULD BE COOL.

SPEAKING OF WEIRD, THERE'S SELA.

SHE'S BARELY SAID TEN SENTENCES TO ANY OF US SINCE THE SCHOOL YEAR STARTED.

I KNOW. IT FEELS LIKE SOMETHING'S WRONG, BUT I DON'T KNOW WHAT.

ONCE SOMEONE GOES GOTH, THEY'RE LOST TO THE DARK SIDE.

IF SHE WANTS TO BE MOODY, I SAY LET HER ALONE...

I'M GONNA GO TRY TO TALK TO HER.

8

HEY, SELA. YOU WANT MY MILK?

I DON'T REALLY WANT IT.

SURE. I'LL TAKE YOUR UNWANTED MILK.

IT'LL GO GREAT IN MY COFFEE.

SO... HOW HAVE YOU BEEN?

YOU HAVEN'T REALLY BEEN HANGING OUT WITH US SINCE SCHOOL STARTED AND...

MAYBE I FOUND STRENGTH IN MYSELF AS A PERSON AND DECIDED I DIDN'T NEED TO RELY ON OTHERS FOR SELF-VALIDATION?

OH. OKAY.

WELL, IF YOU EVER WANT TO HANG OUT, OR TALK, OR PLAY CRAFTZONE...

I KNOW WHERE YOUR ARENA IS.

I knew where Sela's arena was too, though I hadn't been there for months. Not since she went out of town for some reason during the summer.

It wasn't a vacation from the looks of things. Or if it was, she came back miserable.

OH! TAY-TAY, YOU'RE HOME EARLY!

NO, NANA. YOU JUST FELL ASLEEP.

I'LL TELL YOU A SECRET. I FELL ASLEEP AT SCHOOL TODAY, TOO. MUST RUN IN THE FAMILY.

CHILD, YOU'RE SLEEPY 'CAUSE ALL YOU DO IS PLAY THOSE SILLY VIDEO GAMES.

WHY DO YOU LET THEM TAKE HOLD OF YOU? YOU USED TO MAKE UP STORIES ALL ON YOUR OWN. YOU WERE SUCH A GOOD STORYTELLER...

NANA, I STILL AM. I JUST DO IT DIFFERENTLY, NOW.

I'VE TOLD YOU BEFORE THAT CRAFTZONE IS A WORLDBUILDING GAME. I CAN BUILD MY OWN ARENAS AND CREATE MY OWN ADVENTURES.

WOULDN'T YOU LIKE TO CREATE YOUR OWN REALITY SOMETIMES?

IN MY AGE, PEOPLE WHO CREATED THEIR OWN REALITY WERE CALLED "SOFT-HEADED"... OR WORSE.

NO DANGER OF THAT FROM ME.

WHOA!

OW! HOW DID THAT HAPPEN IN REALITY?

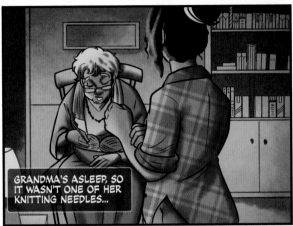

GRANDMA'S ASLEEP, SO IT WASN'T ONE OF HER KNITTING NEEDLES...

WAIT... WHAT?

MOM AND DAD ARE ASLEEP, TOO? BUT IT CAN'T BE THAT LATE?

WHATEVER POKED ME, IT SURE STINGS...

KIARA, I'M GOING OVER TO --

...SHE'S ASLEEP, TOO?

WHAT IS GOING ON?

NO SIGNAL

I'D SAY I'M IN A DREAM, BUT THIS IS TOO REAL...

MAYBE ONCE I TALK TO SELA, THIS WILL ALL MAKE SENSE.

15

BING BONG

OKAY, I'M GETTING WEIRDED OUT. OFFICIALLY.

WHAT ARE YOU DOING HERE?

I CAME TO TALK TO YOU.

AND I'M GETTING A SENSE OF DÉJÀ VU.

YOU WERE JUST IN THE GAME, RIGHT? CRAFTZONE ARENA?

YEAH, YOU CAME INTO MY REALM, UNINVITED.

LAST TIME I WAS THERE, I DIDN'T NEED AN INVITE.

AND LAST TIME IT WASN'T A CREEPY THORN WORLD.

AND, ON TOP OF THAT, I GOT HURT FOR REAL IN YOUR REALM.

SO, I THINK WE GOTTA TALK.

OKAY. LET'S GO UP TO MY ROOM.

17

WELCOME TO MY MADNESS.

HOLY... ARE THESE ALL YOURS?

I MEAN, YOU COULD ALWAYS DRAW, BUT THESE ARE NEXT LEVEL!

WHAT, WERE YOU AWAY AT ART SCHOOL THIS SUMMER?

I WISH.

IF ONLY IT WERE THAT COOL.

WHAT ARE YOU HIDING?

JUST TALK TO ME! WE USED TO BE ABLE TO TALK ALL THE TIME...

YOU KNOW HOW I'VE HAD A LOT OF MOODY MOMENTS LAST YEAR, AND THEY WERE GETTING WORSE?

THEY GOT REALLY BAD RIGHT AFTER SCHOOL ENDED.

THE DOCTORS TESTED MY THYROID, BUT IT WASN'T THAT.

I.... I'M BIPOLAR.

WHAT DOES THAT MEAN?

IT MEANS THAT I HAVE MANIC EPISODES WHERE I'M FEELING SO GOOD THAT I'M HYPER AND TALK FAST, AND DON'T SLEEP.

BUT MOSTLY, I'VE BEEN HAVING DEPRESSIVE EPISODES.

MY ENERGY IS GONE, I FEEL WORTHLESS, AND I FEEL GUILTY AND UNWANTED.

MOST OF THE TIME, I DON'T WANT TO BE ANYWHERE WHERE THERE ARE PEOPLE AT ALL. I JUST WANT THE WORLD TO BE QUIET.

IS THAT WHY YOU CHANGED YOUR ARENA IN THE GAME? BUT WHY DID IT LOOK LIKE IT WAS ATTACKING YOU?

IT'S LIKE MY BRAIN IS FIGHTING ITSELF ALL THE TIME.

THE MORE I TRY TO GET BETTER, THE MORE IT FIGHTS ME.

19

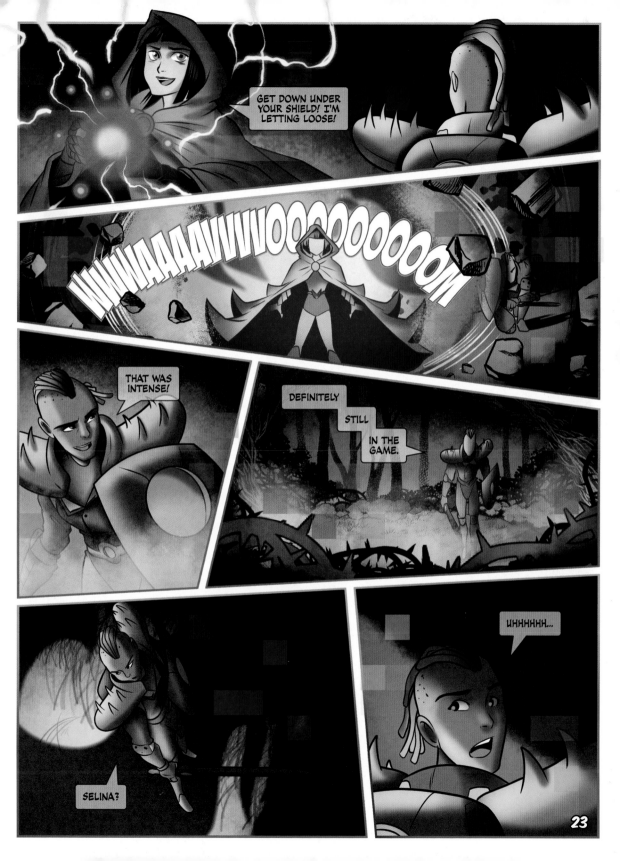

WHAAA...

NANA?

SO YOU'RE FINALLY AWAKE, HUH?

CHILD, YOU WERE HAVING SOME CRAZY DREAM.

YOU WERE CHATTERING AWAY ABOUT THE GAME NONSTOP AFTER YOU TOOK YOUR FORTY WINKS.

WAIT... WAS IT ALL A DREAM?

GIRL, I TRIED TO WAKE YOU UP.

EVEN POKED YOU IN THE ARM WITH ONE OF MY KNITTING NEEDLES, BUT YOU ARE SO SLEEP-DEPRIVED, YOU JUST STAYED SNOOZING!

I THINK I HAVE TO SEE A FRIEND RIGHT NOW.

I GOTTA GO, NANA. I LOVE YOU.

WHAT ABOUT YOUR GAME?

So far so good.

This definitely looks more lively.

HEY... SELA...

I WAS WONDERING IF YOU WERE GOING TO COME OVER.

I WAS ALSO WONDERING IF ANY OF IT WAS REAL.

I DON'T KNOW WHAT IT WAS.

DID WE SHARE A DREAM? WERE WE HALLUCINATING?

OR WAS IT ALL SOME DEEP DISCUSSION WE HAD IN THE GAME.

LIKE, IF WE CHECK THE SAVED DATA LOGS, WAS IT ALL JUST GAMEPLAY?

EITHER WAY, WAS WHAT YOU TOLD ME TRUE?

ABOUT YOUR BIPOLAR DISORDER?

YEAH. UNFORTUNATELY SO.

BUT WHATEVER THAT ADVENTURE WAS, YOU MADE ME UNDERSTAND THAT I DON'T WANT EVERYONE TO GO AWAY.

AND I DON'T WANT ME... TO GO AWAY, EITHER.

WILL YOU HELP ME, TAY?

LIKE, MAKE SURE I TAKE MY MEDS AND STAY ON THE RIGHT TRACK?

ABSOLUTELY!

BUT I DON'T THINK IT'S JUST PILLS THAT ARE GOING TO HELP YOU...

I'VE GOT A GREAT IDEA HOW WE CAN CHANNEL SOME OF THAT WEIRDNESS THAT'S INSIDE BOTH OF US, INSTEAD OF JUST ESCAPING REALITY IN A GAME...

THE MARVEL UNIVERSE IS ABSOLUTELY BETTER, CINEMATICALLY AND IN THE COMICS.

NO WAY. THE DC UNIVERSE HAS BEEN AROUND WAY LONGER, AND LOOK AT HOW MANY TV SHOWS THEY HAVE --

MOVE OVER, NERD!

WHAT? UH... HUH?

HHHHHIIIIISSSSSS

AAAHHH!

HA HA HA HA!

THANK YOU, HECTOR.

SO... ARE YOU, LIKE, NORMAL NOW, SELA?

NOBODY AT THIS TABLE IS NORMAL, MATT.

YOU GOT CHEST HAIR WHEN YOU WERE 12!

SELA AND I HAD AN INTERESTING WEEKEND.

WE WORKED OUT A LOT OF STUFF...

AND WE WORKED ON SOMETHING NEW, INSTEAD OF JUST GAMING...

THESE TWO LOOK A LITTLE FAMILIAR...

MY NANA SAYS TO "WRITE WHAT YOU KNOW."

SHE'S ALSO BEEN AFTER ME TO PUT MY STORYTELLING TO GOOD USE.

AND SINCE SELA'S AN AWESOME ARTIST, WE THOUGHT WE'D TRY OUR HANDS AT COMIC BOOKS!

TO BRIGHTER DAYS AHEAD!

TO BRIGHTER DAYS, TAY!

...THE END... FOR NOW!

WHAT DO YOU THINK?

ESCAPING FROM THE WORLD AROUND US IS NORMAL. WHEN WE'RE YOUNG, WE DO THIS BY READING, WATCHING TV, OR PLAYING GAMES. BUT IT'S IMPORTANT NOT TO ALLOW THIS TO OVERWHELM REALITY. AS WE GROW, WE HAVE MORE RESPONSIBILITIES AND DECISIONS TO MAKE. THE THINGS WE CAN LEARN IN REALITY HELP WITH THAT. IF YOU PAY ATTENTION TO THE THINGS YOU ESCAPE WITH, AND APPLY SOME OF THE THINGS YOU LEARN TO YOUR REALITY, YOU CAN FIND A GOOD BALANCE!

- Beauté falls asleep in class because she's spending too much time playing games. We've all fallen asleep in class or other places. If you're doing a lot, you aren't getting enough sleep. Have you ever fallen asleep in class? What happened when you woke up? Do you ever stay up late because you want to read one more chapter or play one more game? Were you extra sleepy the next day?

- Sela is isolating herself from her friends, and it shows in the way she acts, the way she dresses, and where she sits in the lunchroom. She's worried about how people will treat her since she knows she is bipolar, but she's making her depression worse. When you're depressed, do you push people away? Have you thought about talking to somebody who might listen? You're never the only person who has feelings like you are feeling, good or bad.

- Tay and Sela escape the world by playing video games, where their actions and adventures have no consequences. That is a common way to deal with stress. When you want to escape, what do you do?

- Tay's grandmother encourages her granddaughter to spend more time writing or doing something other than playing video games. Many of us today play on phones or computers a lot. But what could you do to find fun and adventure in the real world around you?

- Tay and Sela decide to make their own comic book adventures. When we create something from our mind, it can be fun and rewarding. Have you ever made something creative? How did it make you feel?

NEW STORIES & OLD TALES:
FAIRY TALE FUN FACTS

1. Fairy tales are make-believe stories that a storyteller created "once upon a time." The tales became widely known as they were written down. Writers would borrow tales from each other and change or expand them. They kept the basics but put their own kind of magic into the stories.

2. The earliest "Sleeping Beauty" tale was in an anonymous book called "Perceforest." It was written between 1330 and 1344. Charles Perrault adapted his version in 1697. The Brothers Grimm adapted Perrault's tale for their 1812 story, "Little Briar Rose," or "The Sleeping Beauty in the Woods."

3. In all "Sleeping Beauty" stories, a princess falls into an enchanted sleep and must be rescued. Often, the sleep is caused by the princess being poked by a cursed spinning wheel. Everyone in the castle is put to sleep, and brambles and thorns grow around the castle. Later, a prince braves the wall, enters the castle, and kisses Beauty. As she awakens from the kiss, the enchantment ends.

4. "Sleeping Beauty" has been adapted for stage musicals, ballet, animation, film, and television. The most famous version is Walt Disney's 1959 animated film of the same name, which introduced the evil Maleficent. In 2014, Disney released a live-action *Maleficent* film, and a sequel in 2019.

5. Russian composer Pyotr Ilyich Tchaikovsky created the music for a *Sleeping Beauty* ballet. It was first produced in Saint Petersburg, Russia, in 1890. His beloved work is still performed all over the world today. Many people recognize the songs because Disney adapted most of them for its 1959 animated movie and the first *Maleficent* film!

GLOSSARY

Bipolar — Any of several psychological disorders of mood characterized usually by alternating episodes of depression and mania. Also called manic depression, manic-depressive illness.

Cinematic Universe — A set of creative works where more than one writer independently contributes a work that can stand alone but fits into the joint development of the story line, characters, or world of the overall project.

IRL — an abbreviation for "in real life".

Self-Validation — The feeling of having recognized, confirmed, or established one's own worthiness or legitimacy.

Video Games — An electronic game in which players control images on a video screen.

Worldbuilding — The art of creating a new fictional world.

ONLINE RESOURCES

Booklinks
NONFICTION NETWORK
FREE! ONLINE NONFICTION RESOURCES

To learn more about WORLDBUILDING GAMES, BIPOLAR DISORDER, and BULLYING, please visit abdobooklinks.com or scan this QR code. These links are routinely monitored and updated to provide the most current information available.